# Paul Bunyan

Tale retold by Bill Balcziak
Illustrated by Patrick Girouard

Adviser: Dr. Alexa Sandmann, Professor of Literacy,
The University of Toledo; Member, International Reading Association

 **COMPASS POINT BOOKS**
Minneapolis, Minnesota

Compass Point Books
3109 West 50th Street, #115
Minneapolis, MN 55410

Visit Compass Point Books on the Internet at *www.compasspointbooks.com*
or e-mail your request to *custserv@compasspointbooks.com*

Photograph ©: Jim Wark, 28.

Editor: Catherine Neitge
Designer: Les Tranby

**Library of Congress Cataloging-in-Publication Data**
Balcziak, Bill, 1962-
  Paul Bunyan / written by Bill Balcziak; illustrated by Patrick Girouard.
    p. cm.— (The Imagination Series: Tall tales)
Summary: Presents the life story of the enormous lumberjack, Paul Bunyan, who along with his blue ox Babe,
is said to have made the 10,000 lakes of Minnesota with his footsteps.
  ISBN 0-7565-0459-7 (hardcover)
  ISBN 0-7565-0897-5 (paperback)
  1.  Bunyan, Paul (Legendary character)—Legends. [1. Bunyan, Paul (Legendary character)—Legends.
  2. Folklore—United States. 3. Tall tales.]  I. Title. II. Series.
  PZ8.1.B183 Pau 2003
  398.2'0973'02—dc21                          2002015118

# Table of Contents

## Giant of a Man

It started with some shaking on the forest floor. Squirrels and birds raced for cover. There was a rumble. Then there was a loud bang and a big boom. Trees swayed and danced. Was it a mighty thunderstorm? The once quiet forest was alive with noise. Then, as quickly as it began, the noise stopped. The forest grew quiet.

An enormous man stood in a clearing near a large pond. He was taller than the treetops. His shoulders were as wide as a house. He wore a red flannel shirt and sturdy pants, like the kind worn by lumberjacks. He carried an ax with a handle as long as a pine tree. His big muscles made it clear he could swing the ax very hard. He looked hot and tired, as though he had been working all day.

The man kneeled down and slid his huge hand into the pond. He scooped up some water and drank. "Now that," said the giant, "is the best water I have ever tasted!" He rose up, stretched his arms wide, and turned toward the setting sun. With another explosion of noise, he crashed away through the woods. Just like that, he was gone. The forest grew silent once again.

The legend of Paul Bunyan started in the north woods more than a century ago. Today, nearly everyone knows about this giant, whose adventures took him across North America. The tales about Paul Bunyan are almost as "tall" as the man himself.

## Big Baby Bunyan

Not surprisingly, Paul Bunyan started life as a very, very big baby. How big? It took six strong storks to carry him to his new parents' home in Maine. When he arrived, his mother wept with joy. She loved her big, strong, beautiful baby. When she tried to take him in her arms, however, he weighed so much that she sank in the ground all the way up to her waist.

Baby Paul was always hungry, and he let people know it. He cried so loudly, the sound cracked a man's eyeglasses five miles away.

Paul's mother fed him:
- Ten gallons of milk
- Twenty pancakes
- Thirty pints of berries (He cried for more!)
- Forty pounds of oatmeal
- Fifty slices of bread
- Sixty strips of bacon
- Seventy sausages
- Eighty eggs
- Ninety crackers
- One hundred spoonfuls of applesauce

That was just his breakfast!

Oh, how that baby grew! When the storks brought him, he wore a diaper made from a potato sack. After a week, he outgrew his father's clothes. Within a month, his mother sewed his pants out of blankets and his shirts out of tents.

Little Paul slept in a crib made from a hay wagon. He was rocked to sleep by a team of horses pulling on either side.

One morning Paul slipped out of his crib and rolled down a big hill to the ocean. He tumbled right in. His splashing caused the tide to rise WAY above normal.

By the time his parents dragged him to shore, boats were sunk all along the coast. Villages were flooded, and people were mad! Angry villagers told the Bunyans to raise their big baby someplace else.

## Look at Him Grow

So the Bunyans moved. They made a raft of pine trees and sailed young Paul all the way up the Saint Lawrence River.

People from all around came to see the Bunyan lad grow. "Oh my," they would exclaim, "that boy is mighty big!" By age four, he could reach the tops of small trees. By age six, he was as tall as an oak. At age ten, he stood twice as high as a white pine.

One day, his father decided to build a house closer to the lake.

"Father," Paul said, "why not just move our house rather than build a new one?"

His father shook his head. "It would take a team of forty horses working all day to drag that house to a new spot," he said.

Paul laughed with glee. He reached down and picked up his parents' house in his chubby hands. He carried it more than a mile to a nice, shady place by the water. "There, Father," he said. "Is that a good spot?" His father beamed with pride.

Of course, young Paul was too big to sleep in the house. His father made him a special bed in a large barn nearby. He filled the barn with straw to keep the boy warm during the cold winter nights.

When Paul was twelve, the winter was the coldest anybody had ever seen. Birds froze in midair and stayed there until the spring thaw. People's breath hung in solid, frozen clouds that bumped

their heads if they weren't careful.

One night it got so cold the falling snow turned from white to blue. Blue icicles as big as logs hung everywhere. Blue snow formed huge drifts. The night sky glowed with the color of the snow and the ice and the clouds.

During the night, Paul heard a terrible noise. It sounded like a train—maybe an express—but Paul knew there were no trains running on *this* night. He opened the barn door and stared into the blizzard. He couldn't see anything. "It must be the wind," Paul said to himself. He went back to sleep and tried to keep warm.

The next morning, he bundled up and went outside. The whole world was blue. He walked toward the lake and stopped in front of a huge pile of snow. The strange noise was coming from inside.

Paul started digging. To his surprise, a large brown eye looked up at him through the hole. It blinked. Paul cleared more blue snow. Now he could see two eyes. He dug some more. A pair of horns appeared.

### Babe, the Blue Ox

"It's an ox!" Paul cried. The animal climbed out of the snow, and even Paul was shocked at its size. The ox stood 24 ax handles tall and had strong, wide shoulders.

The poor beast was so cold it had turned as blue as the snow. It cried, and Paul remembered the sound of a train the night before. He covered his ears against the roar.

Paul leaned down to warm the beast. He was surprised when it nuzzled its snout into his arms. After the creature warmed up, Paul stepped back and stared. The ox was still blue! "You're a special animal," said Paul with a smile.

He called the ox "Babe" and they became the very best of friends. No matter where Paul Bunyan's adventures took him, Babe, the Blue Ox, was with him every giant step of the way.

When Paul turned 18, his father made him an ax from the trunk of an ash. The ax head was forged from metal melted down from an old steam engine. "Son," said Mr. Bunyan, "it is time for you to make your way in the world. Go west, and find work in the lumber camps."

Paul and Babe were sad to leave Ma and Pa Bunyan but excited to start a new adventure. Paul tipped his cap to his father and lifted his mother up for a hug. "Paul Bunyan! You put me down right now, you hear?" his mother cried from amid the treetops. But she smiled as she said it.

No sooner had Paul started his journey than he heard gold had been discovered in nearby Michigan! Paul and Babe raced to get there only to find great forests where the gold was supposed to be.

"I'll be hornswoggled," said Paul. Babe snorted.

"Well," said Paul, after they made camp, "let's start looking for that gold." With a single swing of his giant ax, Paul cleared a HUGE area. Soon, thousands of trees had been cleared. There was still no sign of gold.

"I guess we'll just start digging

for the gold, then," he sighed. Paul hitched a plow to Babe and the ox dug in and began to pull. "Pull harder, Babe! Pull!" Paul shouted.

Soon, Babe had dug five huge holes. There was still no gold. Paul and Babe were sad. They left the area and continued their journey west. When the rains came that summer, the five holes filled with water. They became what we now call the Great Lakes!

## Life as a Lumberjack

Paul and Babe settled in Minnesota where Paul ran a lumber camp. It was the biggest camp in the world. The people who worked there had to be *at least* ten feet (three meters) tall. To prove their strength, they had to lift a felled tree over their heads while standing on Babe's shoulders.

The lumberjacks worked hard every day. In the evenings they liked to sit around the fire and eat and drink their fill. Paul hired a cook named Sourdough Sam to prepare meals for the crew. Sam used an enormous griddle to make his famous flapjacks.

To grease the griddle, the lumberjacks tied hunks of bacon to their boots and skated around until the grease was bubbling hot. In addition, it took a dozen loggers working nonstop to cut enough wood to keep the fire going. Sourdough Sam would yell "Hurry, now! Hurry! The fire's about out!" and the workers would throw more logs on the fire.

That first Minnesota winter was hard on the loggers. The snow was so deep they had to dig *down* to find the trees. When the spring melt came, the crew floated the logs downstream on the river current. The Mississippi River had so many turns, however, the logs jammed up.

"I can fix that," said Paul with a wink. "Come on Babe!" Paul tied the end of the river to Babe's tail. The big ox pulled the river until it was completely straight. It stayed straight just long enough for the logs to arrive safely downstream.

Today, when a thunderstorm

rolls through the north woods, people go to their windows hoping to spot Paul Bunyan crashing through the forest. But he's rarely seen anymore. Still, people continue to share many stories about his adventures.

Can't you just imagine how Paul's footprints made each of Minnesota's 10,000 lakes? Isn't it interesting to think of Babe slipping on some ice and skidding across the Dakota Territory? Now you know why the plains are completely flat and treeless! Could it be true?

Or is it a tall tale?

*The many lakes of the Boundary Waters lie on Minnesota's border with Canada.*

# A Wild Old Tale

The legend of Paul Bunyan is one of the oldest and wildest of all the tall tales. Many people believe the tale started in the logging camps of Canada in the 1800s. At that time, loggers spent long, hard winters working in the camps. At night, they would gather around the fire and tell stories. Each man tried to top the last story.

The story of Paul Bunyan may have begun as a true story about an extremely large lumberjack. Over time, and in the course of many stories, Paul Bunyan became the biggest of all the tall tale legends. Eventually, the story made it into a newspaper and Paul Bunyan and Babe, the Blue Ox, became famous around the world.

# North Woods Pancakes

Brrrrrrr! It gets cold in the north woods of Minnesota, Michigan, and Maine. A good breakfast helps you keep warm. Here is a recipe for pancakes that Paul would love! It makes eight servings.

1 1/2 cups all-purpose flour
3 1/2 teaspoons baking powder
1 teaspoon salt
1 tablespoon sugar

1 1/4 cups milk
1 egg
3 tablespoons butter, melted

In a large bowl, sift together the flour, baking powder, salt, and sugar. In a smaller bowl, mix together the milk, egg, and melted butter. Make a well in the center of the dry ingredients and pour in the milk mixture, stirring until smooth. Have an adult help you heat a lightly oiled griddle or frying pan over medium high heat. Pour the batter onto the griddle, using about 1/4 cup for each pancake. Brown on both sides and serve hot with butter and syrup.

# Glossary

**amazement**—great surprise or wonder

**blizzard**—a large snowstorm

**enormous**—very large

**express**—a fast train that makes few stops

**felled**—a tree that has been cut down

**flannel**—wool or cotton cloth often used to make work shirts

**forge**—to form something from metal using heat or a hammer

**Great Lakes**—a group of five connected freshwater lakes that lie along the border between the United States and Canada; they are Lakes Superior, Michigan, Huron, Erie, and Ontario

**hornswoggled**—slang for tricked by underhanded methods

**legend**—a story passed down through the years that may not be completely true

**muscles**—the parts of the body that help you move, lift, or push

**rumble**—a noise like the sound of thunder

**Saint Lawrence River**—a river that runs in North America from the Great Lakes to the Atlantic Ocean

**thaw**—weather that is warm enough to melt snow and ice

## Did You Know?

✗ The first printed Paul Bunyan story appeared in the *Detroit News-Tribune* on July 24, 1910.

✗ There are more than 200 roadside statues of Paul Bunyan in the United States.

✗ A giant statue of Paul Bunyan was built for the Chicago Railroad Fair in 1948. It now stands in Brainerd, Minnesota.

✗ Paul Bunyan appeared on a 32-cent United States postage stamp in 1996.

# Want to Know More?

## At the Library

Jensen, Patsy and Jean Pidgeon. *Paul Bunyan and His Blue Ox.* New York: Troll Communications, 1997.

Kellogg, Steven. *Paul Bunyan.* New York: William Morrow and Co., 1985.

Osborne, Mary Pope. *American Tall Tales.* New York: Scholastic, 1991.

Spies, Karen. *Our Folk Heroes.* Brookfield, Conn.: The Millbrook Press, 1994.

Walker, Paul Robert. *Big Men, Big Country: A Collection of American Tall Tales.* New York: Harcourt, 1999.

## On the Web

For more information on *Paul Bunyan,* use FactHound to track down Web sites related to this book.

1. Go to
   *www.compasspointbooks.com/facthound*
2. Type in this book ID: 0756504597
3. Click on the *Fetch It* button.

Your trusty FactHound will fetch the best Web sites for you!

## Through the Mail

**Bemidji: The Home of Paul Bunyan**
Bemidji Visitors & Convention Bureau
P.O. Box 66
Bemidji, MN 56619
800/458-2223 Ext. 105
To write for information about Paul Bunyan and Babe, the Blue Ox

## On the Road

**Paul Bunyan Logging Camp**
110 Carson Park Drive
Eau Claire, WI 54702-0221
715/835-6200
To visit an interpretive center with an interactive tall tales room and other buildings authentic to the 1900s logging era

# Index

**About the Author**

Bill Balcziak has written a number of books for children. When he is not writing, he enjoys going to plays, movies, and museums. Bill lives in Minnesota with his family under the shadow of Paul Bunyan and Babe, the Blue Ox.

**About the Illustrator**

Patrick Girouard has been drawing and painting for many years. He has illustrated more than fifty books for children. Patrick has two sons, Marc and Max, and a dog called Sam. They all live in Indiana.